LITTLE MISS WHOOPS

Roger Hargreaves

Written and illustrated by
Adam Hargreaves

Little Miss Whoops is one of those people who have accidents all of the time.

She has lots of little accidents, like when she is trying to make lunch and drops the eggs!

Whoops!

And she has big accidents, like when she painted her bedroom and tripped over the paint pot!

Whoops!

Every morning when she makes her cup of tea, she spills the milk, tips over the sugar bowl, drops the teabag, breaks the biscuits, knocks her cup of tea across the table and has to start all over again.

Whoops!

Some days it can take hours before she leaves the house.

Little Miss Whoops really is the most accidental person in the world . . . well not quite.

Little Miss Whoops has a brother, Mr Bump. He is just like his sister, if not worse, but that is another story. (Which you may have read.)

Each year, Little Miss Whoops travels by train to visit her brother for a week.

She set off last Tuesday.

This Tuesday, Mr Bump looked at his clock.

Which was lying on the ground where he had just knocked it over.

His sister was late.

A whole week late!

And why was Little Miss Whoops late?

A whole chapter of accidents, of course!

While her train was waiting in a station, she somehow or other tripped and fell out of the train.

Whoops!

And then she somehow or other tripped and fell into the back of a lorry, which took her to Sea Town.

Whoops!

Where, somehow or other she tripped and fell into a boat which took her to another country.

Whoops!

She had to wait nearly a week to get another boat back . . .

. . . and another lorry . . .

. . . and another train.

Little Miss Whoops was exhausted by the time she finally reached her brother's house.

"I thought you were coming last week," said Mr Bump. "It must have been a long trip."

"It was!" said Little Miss Whoops.

"Would you like a cup of tea?" offered Mr Bump.

And you know what that involved don't you?

They spilt the milk, tipped over the sugar bowl, dropped the tea bags, broke the biscuits and knocked the tea all over the table!

What a mess!

Whoops!

"Oh! Look at the time," cried Little Miss Whoops, knocking over the clock. "I've got to go if I'm to catch my train home!"

She grabbed her suitcase and rushed out of the door.

"Goodbye," she called.

"Goodbye," called back Mr Bump. "See you next year!"

Mr Bump waved from the doorway until she had rounded the corner.

Then he closed the door, but as he did, the door handle came off in his hand!

"Whoops!" said Mr Bump.

Fantastic offers for Little Miss fans!

Collect all your Mr. Men or Little Miss books in these superb durable collectors' cases!
Only £5.99 inc. postage and packing, these wipe-clean, hard-wearing cases will give all your Mr. Men or Little Miss books a beautiful new home!

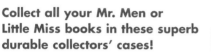

Keep track of your collection with this giant-sized double-sided Mr. Men and Little Miss Collectors' poster.
Collect 6 tokens and we will send you a brilliant giant-sized double-sided collectors' poster! Simply tape a £1 coin to cover postage and packaging in the space provided and fill out the form overleaf.

STICK £1 COIN HERE
(for poster only)

Only need a few Little Miss or Mr. Men to complete your set? You can order any of the titles on the back of the books from our Mr. Men order line on 0870 787 1724. Orders should be delivered between 5 and 7 working days.

───── **TO BE COMPLETED BY AN ADULT** ─────

To apply for any of these great offers, ask an adult to complete the details below and send this whole page with the appropriate payment and tokens, to: MR. MEN CLASSIC OFFER, PO BOX 715, HORSHAM RH12 5WG

☐ Please send me a giant-sized double-sided collectors' poster.
AND ☐ I enclose 6 tokens and have taped a £1 coin to the other side of this page.

☐ Please send me ☐ Mr. Men Library case(s) and/or ☐ Little Miss library case(s) at £5.99 each inc P&P

☐ I enclose a cheque/postal order payable to Egmont UK Limited for £..............

OR ☐ Please debit my MasterCard / Visa / Maestro / Delta account (delete as appropriate) for £..............

Card no. ☐☐☐☐ ☐☐☐☐ ☐☐☐☐ ☐☐☐☐ ☐☐☐☐ Security code ☐☐☐

Issue no. (if available) ☐ Start Date ☐☐/☐☐/☐☐ Expiry Date ☐☐/☐☐/☐☐

Fan's name: Date of birth:

Address:

                                               Postcode:

Name of parent / guardian:

Email for parent / guardian:

Signature of parent / guardian:

Please allow 28 days for delivery. Offer is only available while stocks last. We reserve the right to change the terms of this offer at any time and we offer a 14 day money back guarantee. This does not affect your statutory rights. Offers apply to UK only.

☐ We may occasionally wish to send you information about other Egmont children's books.
If you would rather we didn't, please tick this box.

Ref: LIM 001

Cut along the dotted line and return this whole page